Buster Makes
the Grade

A Marc Brown ARTHUR Chapter Book

Buster Makes the Grade

Text by Stephen Krensky

Based on a teleplay by Peter Hirsch

Little, Brown and Company

Boston   New York   London

First Edition

The characters and events portrayed in this book are fictitious. Any
similarity to real persons, living or dead, is coincidental and not intended
by the author.

Arthur® is a registered trademark of Marc Brown.

Text has been reviewed and assigned a reading level by Laurel S. Ernst,
M.A., Teachers College, Columbia University, New York, New York;
reading specialist, Chappaqua, New York

Library of Congress Cataloging-in-Publication Data

Krensky, Stephen.
    Buster makes the grade / text by Stephen Krensky ; based on a
teleplay by Peter Hirsch. — 1st ed.
        p.   cm. — (A Marc Brown Arthur chapter book ; 16)
    Summary: Arthur and his friends help Buster study for an important
test so that he will be able to move on to the fourth grade with them.
    ISBN 0-316-11960-1 (hc) — ISBN 0-316-12277-7 (pb)
    [1. Schools Fiction.   2. Rabbits Fiction.   3. Aardvark Fiction.
4. Animals Fiction.]   I. Title.   II. Series: Krensky, Stephen. Marc
Brown Arthur chapter book; 16.
PZ7.K883Bu   1999
[Fic] — dc21   99-18410

10 9 8 7 6 5 4 3 2 1

WOR (hc)
COM-MO (pb)

Printed in the United States of America

For dear friends—
Will and Karel Henry

Buster Makes
the Grade

Chapter 1

Mr. Ratburn was handing back some math quizzes to his class.

"A vast improvement, Mr. Barnes," he said to Binky. "Your answers may not always be correct, but I appreciate your neat numbering."

Binky beamed.

Sue Ellen was next. "Coming along," Mr. Ratburn told her. "But I don't think you should draw little pictures in the margins even if you do have extra time."

Sue Ellen blushed.

Mr. Ratburn approached the cluster of desks belonging to Francine, Muffy,

Arthur, and Buster. They were sitting up perfectly straight, with their hands folded in front of them. They were also holding their breath.

"Ms. Frensky, superb . . . you have definitely been practicing. Ms. Crosswire, not bad . . . but you should break the habit of putting lines through your fives. They are not dollar signs. As for you, Mr. Read, I suggest you review those multiplication tables. . . . They can be the best of *times* or the worst of *times*."

Mr. Ratburn stopped for a moment, staring at the last paper.

"And here's yours, Mr. Baxter. . . ."

He gave it to him without further comment. Ordinarily, Buster would have been pleased to be spared one of Mr. Ratburn's remarks. But no comment at all seemed to feel even worse.

As Buster looked at the results, his ears

quivered. Then he quickly folded up the quiz and put it in his pocket.

"Are you okay?" Arthur whispered to him.

Buster waved away his concern. "Fine. Great. Wonderful. Couldn't be better."

Arthur stared at him. "Well, you sure don't look like it."

"Allergies," said Buster. "Nothing to worry about."

Mr. Ratburn returned to the front of the class.

"A few of you should be pleased with your test results. The rest of you can still do better. More than most subjects, math requires us to understand concepts and pay attention to details. Some of you seemed to have forgotten this. I'm reminding you because next Friday we will be having a math test on everything we've learned so far this year."

The whole class groaned.

Buster raised his hand.

"Yes, Mr. Baxter?" said Mr. Ratburn.

"When you say 'everything,' " Buster said, "does that mean *everything?*"

Mr. Ratburn nodded. "Yes. And we already have several months of math behind us. Therefore, I suggest that you begin studying this weekend. Class dismissed."

Everyone got up to leave. But as Buster headed for the door, Mr. Ratburn called out to him.

"Mr. Baxter? Could I see you for a moment?"

Buster slunk over to his teacher's desk. Mr. Ratburn fiddled with some papers until everyone else had left.

"You need to go to the principal's office," said Mr. Ratburn. "Mr. Haney is expecting you."

Buster sighed. Going to the principal's office was not good news. Not good at all.

Chapter 2

· · · · · · · · · · ·

As Buster approached the principal's office, the hall seemed to get longer and longer.

Buster was walking through a long, dark tunnel.

"It's nice down here," Buster said to himself. "Peaceful."

Far ahead was a light at the end of the tunnel. Someone was standing in the light, waving to Buster.

"Come on, Buster. Hurry up!"

Buster couldn't tell who was calling to him, but he had the feeling it would be more comfortable to stay where he was.

"Don't mind me," he called out. *"I'm fine right here."*

"Buster, come here this minute," Ms. Tingley said sternly.

Buster reached the principal's door and stopped.

"You can go right in," Ms. Tingley told him. "They're waiting for you."

"It's always darkest before the dawn, Buster," said Mr. Ratburn, who had just caught up to him. "Let's go inside."

Buster opened the door. He expected to see Mr. Haney because, of course, this was his office. But he did not expect to see anyone else.

Mr. Haney, however, had company.

"Mom! Grandma! What are you doing here?"

Mrs. Baxter dabbed at her eyes with a handkerchief. "It's nothing to worry about, dear," she said nervously.

Then she began to cry.

It was bad enough to think of his mother crying because she had bumped her head or scraped her knee. But to see her cry in the principal's office was more than Buster could bear.

"It'll be okay," he told her. "I don't think Mr. Haney can really make you write anything a hundred times. . . ."

The principal cleared his throat. "Mr. Baxter, your mother isn't crying on her own behalf."

"Oh," Buster said quietly.

Buster's grandmother patted his mother on the back. "There, there," she said softly.

Mr. Ratburn reached for a box of tissues and passed it to Buster's mother.

"Really, Mrs. Baxter," he said, clearing his throat. "It's not as bad as . . . " He turned to Buster. "Although this *is* serious. . . ." He turned back to Buster's mother. "But nothing a little elbow

grease"—he looked at Buster again—"or maybe *a lot* of elbow grease can't fix."

Buster's ears began to droop.

Mr. Haney frowned. "Mr. Baxter, you have come to a turning point, a juncture, a pivotal moment in your young life. The choices you make now will have a lasting effect on your academic career. Therefore, these are not choices to make lightly." Mr. Haney pointed to a chair by his desk. "Er . . . sit down, Buster. We have a lot to talk about."

Chapter 3

• • • • • • • • • • •

Buster was sitting on a swing at the playground when Francine, Arthur, and Muffy found him.

"Buster, we've been looking all over for you," said Francine.

"Oh?" said Buster. "Well, here I am."

"What happened at the principal's office?" Arthur asked. "Is everything okay?"

"Not exactly," said Buster. He told them the whole story.

"At the end, Mr. Ratburn said I had to get a B on the test next week or else."

"Or else?" said Muffy.

"Or else," said Buster, imitating Mr.

Ratburn's voice, "you won't have the pleasure of joining your friends in the fourth grade next year."

"What?" said Arthur. "That's terrible, Buster!"

"Actually," said Francine, "it's a pretty good imitation of Mr. Ratburn."

"Not that," said Arthur. "I mean what he *said.*" He shook his head. "How can we possibly go to fourth grade without you?"

Buster shrugged. "You may have no choice. I don't know enough math to figure out the odds, but my chances can't be good. I mean, I can barely name all thirty states in the country."

"Buster!" said Muffy. "There are fifty states."

Buster sighed. "See how dumb I am? It's hopeless."

"Don't give up yet," said Arthur. "You still have time . . ."

"You sound like my mother and grandmother. Or you would if you were wiping your eyes and blowing your nose in between every other word."

Arthur folded his arms. "Well, if everybody's saying the same thing, what does that tell *you?*"

"I don't know," said Buster. "I don't seem to be very good at thinking lately."

"Maybe you'll feel better after a snack," said Muffy.

"Good idea," said Francine. "Let's get something to eat."

Buster perked up. "It couldn't hurt," he admitted.

The Sugar Bowl was crowded. While they were waiting for a table, Buster walked over to say hello to some other friends.

"Look!" said Francine. "He seems so relaxed. He's not even worried."

"At least not on the outside," said Arthur.

"At this rate," said Muffy, "Buster will fail that test for sure. He'll never get out of third grade."

Arthur nodded.

A grown-up Arthur was returning to his former third-grade class to visit. The kids all looked very small to him. It was hard to believe he had ever been that size.

Sitting among the kids, however, was one person his size. It was Buster — older but apparently not wiser.

Mr. Ratburn pointed at Buster with his cane.

"Mr. Baxter, if a boy is eight years old and repeats third grade thirty-three times, how old would he be now?"

Buster scratched one of his ears. "Uh . . . that's a hard one, Mr. Ratburn. Can I get back to you on that?"

Mr. Ratburn sighed. "Well, there's always next year."

"Earth to Arthur!" said Francine. "Come in, Arthur."

Arthur blinked. "Sorry," he said. He looked out the window and saw Binky walking down the street.

"Wait!" he said. "I know just the person to help us."

Chapter 4

• • • • • • • • • • •

"You want me to *what?*" said Binky.

He blinked at Arthur, Francine, and Muffy, who had come running out of the Sugar Bowl to talk to him.

"We want you to help Buster do better in school," Arthur said again.

Binky laughed. "Me? Help Buster?" He looked down at his arms and legs. "Do I look like the Brain to you? Oh, I get it. This is some kind of joke. You're kidding me, right?"

Arthur looked a little uncomfortable. "Well, no, actually we're very serious. Buster is in danger of having to stay back a year. Since you have, um, some experience in this area . . ."

"We thought you might have some suggestions," Francine added.

Binky frowned for a moment. "Wait a minute. Just because I stayed back doesn't make me an expert." He paused. "Or maybe it does."

"More expert than the rest of us," said Muffy.

"Do you have a special method for learning hard things?" asked Arthur.

"Or some really good books?" asked Francine.

Binky shook his head. "No, nothing like that. Let me think . . . the wheels are turning . . . turning." He smiled. "I know exactly what Buster needs."

"Tell us," said Arthur.

"A tutor!" said Binky. "A private teacher. Mine's Mr. Bagelman. He comes to my house every week to help me study.

His specialty is turning math problems into sports stories. I like those the best."

"A tutor, huh?" said Muffy. "Binky, that's perfect. You're a genius."

Binky blushed. "Oh, I wouldn't say that—but you can if you want."

"Do you think Mr. Bagelman would have time for Buster?" asked Francine. "It's kind of an emergency."

"He might. But there's one thing Mr. Bagelman says over and over again: 'Learning is a two-way street. I can only help you if you want to be helped.'"

"Well, that shouldn't be a problem for Buster," said Arthur. "At least I hope not. Thanks, Binky."

Arthur, Francine, and Muffy went back to the Sugar Bowl to give Buster the news. But Buster was gone.

"Maybe he went to the library," said Francine. "To study."

They checked the library. Buster wasn't there.

Finally they found him in the park, playing on the swings.

"A tutor, huh?" said Buster after they had explained the idea to him. "Sounds great, I guess. Except tutors are expensive, aren't they?"

Nobody knew for sure.

"Besides," said Buster, "I don't know if I'd be comfortable with a stranger." He looked up. "Oh, a game of kickball is starting. See you later."

Buster ran off to the field, leaving his friends staring after him.

"It's never going to work," said Francine. "I don't think learning is a two-way street with Buster. He's making every excuse he can think of."

Muffy sighed. "So all we have to do is find a tutor he knows who is willing to work for free."

"And right away, too," Francine reminded them. "What are the chances of that?"

"Actually," said Arthur, smiling, "I can think of three tutors who fit that description."

"You can?" said Francine. "Who are they?"

"I'm staring at two of them," said Arthur.

"You mean us?" said Francine. "You think one of us can manage the job?"

"Not one of us," Arthur explained. "All of us!"

Everyone looked at one another.

"Yeah!" they shouted together.

Chapter 5

• • • • • • • • • • • •

"Buster, wake up!"

Mrs. Baxter was shaking her son's shoulder without success. Buster clutched his stuffed tiger more tightly and hugged his blankets around him.

"Come on, Buster. You need to get up."

"Why?" It was Saturday. Saturday was not a day when he *needed* to get up.

"Your math tutor is here."

Buster opened his eyes and sat up. "My *what?*"

Then he saw Arthur standing in the doorway.

"Oh," he said, smiling. "It's just you, Arthur."

Mrs. Baxter headed for the door. "It's nice of Arthur to volunteer his time this way. Well, I'll leave you two to your work."

Buster hopped out of bed. "Hey, Arthur, that was a good plan."

"What do you mean?" Arthur asked.

Buster took a quick look in the hall to make sure his mother was gone.

"I mean," he said, "the way you mentioned that tutor stuff. You fooled her completely."

He began digging through the toys and clothes on the floor.

"I know that kickball is here somewhere," he muttered. "If we hurry, we can get to the park before the game starts."

Arthur shook his head. "We're not going to the park today," he said.

"What?"

Arthur dropped some books he was carrying onto the bed.

"I wasn't trying to fool your mother," he said.

"You weren't?"

"Get your books," Arthur ordered. "We're going to study."

Buster's mouth dropped open. For once, he was speechless.

A short while later, Arthur was sitting on Buster's bed, watching Buster work at his desk. Actually, Buster was slumped over a little. His head was buried in a book.

Then Buster let out a loud snore.

"Buster, wake up!" snapped Arthur.

"Huh?"

"You fell asleep again."

"Oh. Sorry." Buster flipped a page. "The world has too many numbers," he muttered. His head began to droop again.

"Buster!"

Buster's head jerked up.

"You've got to stay awake," Arthur told him. "This math book is on the test, and you've barely gotten through a single chapter."

Buster yawned. "It's this room, Arthur. It makes me sleepy. Maybe if we studied outside . . ."

Buster sat at the base of a tree, next to Arthur. A book was open on his lap, but Buster's attention was on a baseball game nearby.

"You're out!" the umpire shouted.

"Buster," said Arthur, "you aren't paying attention."

"Sure I am," said Buster, his eyes never leaving the field. "He was safe. That was a bad call."

"Paying attention to the book, I mean,"

said Arthur. "Come on — you have to do this."

Buster turned back to him. "I know, I know. . . . It's just so hard to keep my eyes on the page. Hey, why don't you read the word problems to me? Then I can really concentrate."

"All right," said Arthur. He took the book and began reading.

"Laura and Owen were making three pies. They started with three cups of flour and three eggs. However . . ."

Arthur looked up.

Buster was gone. He was standing behind the backstop, yelling at the umpire.

Arthur sighed. Getting through to Buster was not going to be easy.

Chapter 6

● ● ● ● ● ● ● ● ● ● ●

During lunch on Monday, Arthur, Binky, Francine, and Muffy huddled around a cafeteria table.

"I tried my best," said Arthur. "But I couldn't get Buster interested in studying."

Francine looked at Buster standing in the lunch line. He was trying to convince Mrs. MacGrady to give him some extra chocolate pudding. "He's not even worried about the big test," she said.

"Of course not," said Muffy. "Nothing affects his appetite. The only thing on Buster's mind is getting two desserts for the price of one."

Francine suddenly brightened. "That's it!" she cried. "The way to Buster's brain is through his stomach. This is what we need to do. . . ."

Later, on the playground, Buster sat with Francine and Muffy. He kept looking around, though, to see if he was missing anything.

"I hope you have a good reason for asking me here," said Buster. "I'm sure I could find a good game somewhere."

Francine just smiled. "Muffy and I bought a bag of double-dipped peanut-fudge swirls. We want to share them with you."

"Really?" Buster beamed. "That's a great reason. I love those things!"

"We know," said Muffy. "And they weren't cheap."

Suddenly Buster frowned. "Wait a minute! It's not my birthday."

Francine dumped out the chocolates. "Of course not. We're going to use these to teach you about division."

Buster groaned. "I knew there had to be a catch."

"Listen up," Francine went on. "There are twenty pieces of candy here. Now, if you and I were going to split them, how many would we each get?"

Buster thought for a moment. Then he gave ten pieces to Francine and kept ten for himself.

"Right!" said Francine. "That's dividing by two."

"Good," said Buster. "Can we eat now?"

Francine shook her head. "Not yet," she said. "Now, what if you want to divide the chocolates by three, so that Muffy gets some, too?"

Buster thought again for a moment. Then he took five chocolates from Francine's pile and gave them to Muffy.

"No," said Muffy. "These piles aren't even."

"Oh," said Buster. "Do they have to be even? You didn't mention that."

Francine stared at him. "Well, I'm mentioning it now," she said.

"Hmmm. All this thinking is making me hungry." Before either girl could stop him, Buster popped a chocolate into his mouth.

"Does that help?" he asked.

"No!" said Muffy. "That's not what we meant. Besides, you still have too many."

"Count carefully," said Francine.

Buster shrugged. He ate another chocolate. "I'll just keep going until you tell me to stop."

"That's not the plan, Buster!" said Muffy.

"But it works!" Buster mumbled, his mouth now full of chocolates.

"Buster, you're impossible!" cried Muffy.

"There will be nothing left to divide if you don't stop."

"I like subtraction better, anyway," said Buster, picking up another chocolate.

"But—"

"Don't bother, Muffy," Francine said sadly. "I thought his stomach would lead to his brain." She sighed. "But I think they're both the same thing."

Chapter 7

• • • • • • • • • • •

At the playground on Wednesday afternoon, Arthur, Binky, Francine, and Muffy were hanging from the monkey bars.

"There are only two days left before the test," said Muffy. "It's time to take drastic action."

"It's about time," said Binky, pounding his right fist against his left hand. "Leave it to me. I know how to make him pay attention."

"You'd probably tie him to a tree," said Francine.

Binky nodded. "A big tree," he added.

"I wish it were that simple," said

Francine. "But Buster's a tough nut to crack."

"The problem," said Arthur, "is that Buster isn't really trying. I made a copy of the multiplication table for him, but he just started drawing on it. He turned all the numbers into animals."

"And let's not forget how he hid a calculator up his sleeve at my house," said Muffy. "We can't help Buster if he won't help himself."

"Sssssh!" said Francine. "Here he comes now."

Buster trudged up to them, his shoulders stooped, his ears drooping. He did not look very happy.

"What's the matter, Buster?" asked Binky. "Couldn't find a game today?"

"It's not that," said Buster. "It's the test. I'm doomed."

"We tried to help," said Francine. "But you were always falling asleep—"

"Or looking for shortcuts," said Muffy.

"I know," said Buster. "I was just hoping the problem would go away somehow if I pretended it didn't really exist. But here we are, and the test is two days away."

"Well," said Arthur, "you still have tonight and tomorrow . . ."

"To learn everything," Buster reminded him.

"Don't worry, Buster," said Binky. "Third grade is a lot easier the second time around." He paused. "Or the third."

Later, Buster and Arthur walked home together.

"Just remember, Buster," said Arthur, "I'll always be your friend. Even when the other fourth graders are picking on you."

"Thanks."

"And we'll still get to see each other in the lunch line."

Buster kicked a stone. "I guess."

They had come to the corner of Main and Water Streets. Buster was going one way and Arthur the other.

"I'm sure going to miss you," said Arthur. "So long, Buster."

As Arthur walked away, Buster heard Binky's words again in his mind: "Third grade is a lot easier the second time around. Or the third."

Outside the principal's office, a very old Buster walked up to the secretary.

"I'm here to see the principal," he croaked.

She waved him into the office. The principal was sitting in a big leather chair, looking out the window with his back to Buster.

Buster cleared his throat.

The principal swiveled around. "Ah, Buster, glad you could get here so quickly."

"I do my best, Arthur," said Buster, eyeing his former friend who was now all grown up.

"I have good news for you, Buster," said Principal Arthur.

"Hooray!" cried Buster, slapping his knee. "I can move up to fourth grade at last?"

Principal Arthur shook his head. "I said good news, not great news. No, actually, we're moving you down to preschool, where you can nap and play all day."

"Please, Arthur, don't do it! I can do better! I know I can!"

Chapter 8

• • • • • • • • • • •

"I know I can," Buster said aloud as he came to his front door. A determined look settled on his face.

Buster went straight to his room and took out all the books from his backpack. He placed them carefully on his desk.

"That's a good start," said a voice inside him. *"Maybe you should take a break."*

Buster shook the thought out of his head.

"Division first," he said, and attacked a set of practice problems. The first one asked him to divide some fruit into three equal groups.

"You don't really care about fruit," said the

voice inside him. *"You should skip the prob- lems about things you don't care about."*

But Buster knew he would not be able to skip problems he didn't like on the test. Besides, this problem reminded him of what Francine and Muffy had tried to teach him with the chocolates.

"Why not use a calculator?" said the voice again.

Buster was tempted. A calculator would make things easier, but he resisted the urge. He wouldn't have a calculator to use during the test, so it wouldn't really help to use one now.

His mother came in twice to check on him, but Buster barely looked up from his books. It was late when he finished all the problems. He was so tired, he fell asleep with his clothes on.

The next day, Buster yawned all through recess.

"You look tired, Buster," said Arthur.

"I am," said Buster. "I was up late studying."

Binky laughed. "That's a good one, Buster. I'm glad you haven't lost your sense of humor."

Buster wanted to argue with him, but he was too tired to bother.

After school, Buster refused an offer to play baseball.

"What's the matter?" his friends asked. "Are you feeling okay?"

Buster didn't want anyone to laugh at him. So he just said he had some other things to do.

Then he went home to study some more.

His books were now spread out all over his desk, his bed, and the floor. But Buster knew where everything was, and he moved from one topic to the next with computer-like precision.

Mrs. Baxter wanted Buster to take a break for dinner, but Buster wouldn't stop. So his mother brought him his meal on a tray. For dessert, there were some small round candies in assorted colors.

Buster was about to eat them when he paused for a moment. Then he separated the candies into color-coordinated groups.

"I'll eat them," he said, "after I understand this next part about groups and sets."

Hours passed before the candies were eaten and Buster got ready for bed. He had done everything he could, even if he had crammed a bit at the end.

When his mother came in to say good night, Buster was already asleep. He had a smile on his face, though, and she took that as a good sign.

Chapter 9

● ● ● ● ● ● ● ● ● ● ●

The morning of the big test, Buster was up and dressed before his mother came in to wake him.

"Why, Buster," she said, "aren't you an eager beaver today."

Buster finished tying his sneakers. "Not eager, exactly," he admitted, "but ready, I hope."

"Well, come into the kitchen. I've got breakfast on the table."

Buster didn't have much of an appetite, but his mother made him eat anyway.

"If your stomach is grumbling during

your test," she said, "you won't be able to hear yourself think."

Buster tried to eat, but he cut up his toast into squares, pushing them around on his plate.

"What interesting patterns," his mother commented.

"It's geometry," Buster explained.

His mother nodded. "Well, just make sure you eat all of your geometry before it gets cold."

On the way to school, Buster mumbled to himself, going over his multiplication tables. A new house was going up along his route, and normally Buster stopped to check its progress. This morning the cement trucks were pouring the foundation, but Buster paid no attention. He was too busy going over his fives and sixes to notice.

At the next intersection, Francine and Arthur were waiting for the light to change.

"Isn't that Buster?" said Francine. "HEY, BUSTER! CATCH UP TO US!"

Buster didn't look up.

"Why isn't he answering?" asked Francine.

Arthur shrugged. "I don't think he heard you. He looks deep in thought."

"Deep in thought?" said Francine. "This is Buster we're talking about, remember?" She took another look. "He does seem distracted. . . . Oh, well, I guess he'll get to school on his own."

Buster was sitting at a small table in a giant warehouse. He was sorting a pile of numbers jumbled together. All along the walls were stacks of facts and numbers in every shape and size. Many were covered with a thick layer of dust. They looked like they had not been moved in many years.

A supervisor wearing a hard hat and a long white coat came over to inspect Buster's work.

"You must work faster, Buster," said Mr. Ratburn. "This information has been neglected for far too long."

"I'm doing my best," Buster told him. "A lot of the work has piled up over time."

"And whose fault is that?" asked Mr. Ratburn. "Well, don't stop now. As you can see," he added, pointing to the walls around them, "you have a long way to go."

Buster blinked when he reached the park. He had come to the end of the nines.

"Nine times nine is . . . eighty-one!" he shouted, leaping up onto a park bench. "I did it!"

A flock of birds scattered from the tree overhead, and several people stopped to stare.

Buster didn't care. In less than one hour,

he would be sitting at his desk up to his ears in test questions. But that was okay.

He was ready at last.

Chapter 10

• • • • • • • • • • • •

Mr. Ratburn stood at his desk holding a pile of papers. In front of him, the class grew suddenly quiet.

"I have graded last week's tests," he announced. "Most of them were very good. But not all. Some of you may be a little disappointed."

Everyone looked a little nervous — everyone except Buster. He looked absolutely terrified. All the hairs on his head were standing up as straight as his ears.

Arthur put a hand on his friend's shoulder. "You gave it your best shot, Buster. That's all you could do."

Buster sighed.

"Look on the bright side," said Francine. "I hear the second graders have a great baseball team."

"And you'll have an easy time bossing them around," Binky pointed out.

Mr. Ratburn walked down the aisle, handing back the tests.

"Good job, Sue Ellen. . . . Not bad, Fern. . . . Creative answers, Muffy."

When he came to Buster, he stopped.

"Well, Mr. Baxter, I understand you put in a lot of hard work for this test."

Buster nodded. At that moment he was unable to speak.

"Hard work is the backbone of this country," Mr. Ratburn went on. "But it must be focused and disciplined in order to produce results."

Buster could hear his heart pounding in his chest.

"In this case, your hard work paid off—

handsomely." Mr. Ratburn handed Buster his test. "Congratulations! You got a miraculous, but well-deserved, B+."

Everyone cheered.

"You did it, Buster!" cried Arthur.

"Amazing," said Francine.

"And without spending a dime," observed Muffy.

Mr. Ratburn then handed Arthur his test. "I don't want to spoil the moment," he said, "but you, Mr. Read, need to work on your division." He paused. "Perhaps Mr. Baxter could give you a few pointers."

"Sure," said Buster. "I'd be glad to. You see, Arthur, it's all in how you split up the colored candy. . . ."

He continued to explain even after the bell rang, following Arthur out the door to their lockers. And for once, Arthur didn't try to stop him. If he had learned anything this past week, it was that Buster had a mind of his own.

F
KRE

Krensky, Stephen.

Buster makes the
grade.

20120

$12.70

F
KRE

Krensky,
Stephen.

Buster makes the
grade.

$12.70

20120

DATE	BORROWER'S NAME	
JAN 02 2004	AWN	K2
APR 10 2001	Laoda	3B
APR 25 2001	Brian	
MAY		

SUNDERLAND ELEMENTARY SCHOOL

Library
Sunderland Elementary School
Sunderland, Massachusetts